Puffin Books

VERA PRATT AND THE BALD HEAD

Vera Pratt and her son Wally enter the Motorbike and Sidecar Grand Prix, to be held near Wally's school.

When Vera's old enemy, Captain Smoothy-Smythe, hears about the first prize of five thousand pounds his criminal mind is set spinning and he dreams up a wicked scheme with the help of the evil Dud Cheque . . . Suddenly Wally has been kidnapped and Vera has to enlist the help of a very reluctant partner in the race.

This is the third hilarious adventure about Vera Pratt and her son Wally. The other books in the series, also published in Puffin, are *Vera Pratt and the False Moustaches* and *Vera Pratt and the Bishop's False Teeth*.

BROUGH GIRLING was born in 1946. His previous jobs include teacher, ice-cream salesman, business man, freelance copy-writer and promotions consultant. As well as writing children's books he is Campaign Director of Readathon, the sponsored reading event that raises money for the Malcolm Sargent Cancer Fund for Children, and is head of the Children's Book Foundation at Book Trust in London.

Contents

I

Mrs Pratt and Son

'What's for breakfast, Mum?' asked Wally Pratt.

'*WALLACE!*' exclaimed Vera Pratt. 'What a ridiculous question to ask a mother. It's not *my* job to tell you what's for breakfast – I've got work to

do! For a start I've got to get this Honda XLC's engine in racing trim by Saturday.'

You can tell from this that Wally's mum is not like those kind, gentle, soppy mothers you see in the ads on television – the ladies who talk to their neighbours about how white their washing is, or pour April-fresh things down the lavatory and smile about it.

Wally sometimes wished that she was a little more like them, but he didn't have time to think about it now because she continued:

'When I was your age I could strip the engine out of a Morris Minor with my eyes closed, and change the gaskets on a tractor with one hand tied behind my back! The limit of your mechanical skill seems to be knowing how to turn the telly on. Don't just stand there like a beached whale with a headache – get your own breakfast! And eat plenty: with this Motorbike and Sidecar Grand Prix at the track on Saturday I want you good and heavy in the sidecar. Ballast, Wally, that's what you're good for – ballast!'

Wally Pratt poured himself a mountain of corn-flakes, added sugar, and tucked in. After a couple of crunchy mouthfuls he summoned up the courage to speak:

'Do I really have to come in the sidecar on Saturday, Mum? It shakes me to bits, that bike of yours

. . . Why can't we get a car and behave like normal people?'

'Don't be a wally, Wally,' said his mother, rolling her eyes towards the ceiling and mopping her brow on her oily pinny. 'There's a five thousand pound first prize. I need the money, and of course I need you in the sidecar. Honestly! Kids today!' She put her hands on her black leather hips. 'I sometimes think you just take me for granted – asking me what's for breakfast and not wanting to help in the sidecar and nonsense like that: I'm a working mother, Wally, not your servant! I spend my life cleaning and mending as it is. I was up all hours last night polishing the rivets on the sidecar nose cone and welding the bike's front forks – and what thanks do I get?!'

Wally Pratt sighed and looked apologetic.

Vera saw this and changed to a calmer tone, trying to reason with her son:

'I've explained before, Wally, cars are inconvenient, especially for a housewife. How could I get a car into the kitchen to recondition its suspension? With a bike it's easy. Now get on with a good hearty meal, and be well prepared for Saturday's race. We've got to win.'

Wally crunched on, and reflected that if your mother is a motorbike fanatic it's probably sensible to accept it and get on with life as best you can.

There was a knock at the front door.

'Go and answer that, Wally, there's a good lad, or I'll never get these carburettors balanced and race-tuned by the weekend.'

Wally went to the door and there, on the step, stood three of his best friends.

I don't know if you've met them before so I'd better introduce them:

Wally's closest friend is a boy called Bean Pole. He may have a more normal, sensible name, but people call him Bean Pole because he is tall, gangling and stringy. He and Wally get on well because they are opposites – like Laurel and Hardy.

You will probably have gathered that Wally is a plump, slow-moving youth who is inclined to be-have like a slug on its day off. Unless there's an emergency – when he can produce an impressive burst of energy – he takes things slowly. Bean Pole, however, is quick and eager. He is the sort of boy who actually prefers doing things to watching TV. Wally finds this difficult to understand but likes Bean Pole in spite of it.

Standing next to Bean Pole that morning was Ginger Tom. He is not a cat: he's a boy called Tom who has carroty red hair and freckles. He is small and resourceful and he thinks and moves fast. If you ever wanted someone to nip through a half-open window in a hurry he'd be the guy to do it.

Bill Stickers is the last of the three. His parents christened him William Stukley but one day when Wally Pratt and Bean Pole saw a notice saying 'Bill Stickers Will Be Prosecuted' they instantly renamed him Bill Stickers. Bill's main problem is that he always looks a mess. His mother spends her life telling him to tuck things in and do his hair and polish his shoes but it makes no difference. He always looks as if he's been put together in a hurry.

So there they are: Bean Pole, Ginger Tom, and Bill Stickers.

'Aren't you ready for school yet, Wally?' asked Bean Pole.

'Oh . . . yeah . . . hang on a minute, I've been having a discussion with my mum.'

'Have you seen the bit in the paper about the Grand Prix?' went on Bean Pole eagerly.

'No,' said Wally, reaching for his school coat.

'It's on the front page – look!' said Bill Stickers pulling the morning newspaper from the top of his already dishevelled trousers and unfolding it for Wally to see.

'It says that your mum is taking part, and that old Edwards has said that all of us have got to help with the arrangements,' added Ginger Tom.

'You what?!' exclaimed Wally. He held up the front page and Bill pointed to a small heading half-way down it:

PUPILS AT ST BERNARD'S TO HELP ON RACE DAY

Mr Edwards, Headteacher at St Bernard's school, has said that all the older pupils will be helping at Saturday's Motorbike and Sidecar Grand Prix. 'Some of the children will help in the car parks and public areas, others will be on pit security or will be assisting track and flag marshals,' said the Headteacher, aged 42. 'It will be a good opportunity for them to be of service to the local community and bring credit to the school.'

'Good, isn't it?' said Ginger Tom. 'I hope I'm a track marshal – maybe I could be the one with the chequered flag at the end of the race.'

'Hang on,' said Wally – it was one of his most common expressions. 'My mum's not going to like this: she wants me in the sidecar as usual.'

'She's mentioned here too,' said Bill Stickers, pointing out a larger column at the top of the page:

As well as many top teams from Europe, local motorbike enthusiast Mrs V. Pratt has registered to enter the race. Officials and organizers hope other local teams will come forward by Wednesday's closing date. 'It would be splendid if the £5,000 first prize was won by someone in the local community,' said Colonel Thundering-Blunderer, Chairman of the Grand Prix Committee.

Wally took the paper through to his mother in the kitchen.

'Look, Mum, you're in the paper again, and Mr Edwards says we've all got to be track marshals and stuff like that.'

'Well you're not, Wally – you'll be beside your mother, where a boy ought to be. I'll write the school a note.'

Vera Pratt put down her adjustable spanner and wiped her hands on a tea towel.

So it was that moments later Wally Pratt set off for school with a letter in his pocket asking the Headteacher to excuse him from official race track duties on Saturday because his mother wanted him as ballast in her sidecar.

2

Down at the ABC Garage

Down at the ABC Garage someone else had read
about the Motorbike and Sidecar Grand Prix in the
morning newspaper: Captain Smoothy-Smythe.

The ABC Garage looks like any other rather
run-down garage. Two old petrol pumps stand on a
forecourt which is pitted with oily puddles, and cars

in various states of repair and decay are parked around the building. Piles of scrap metal, old tyres and dirty oil drums complete the picture.

The workshop, whose entrance is round at the back of the garage, is a dark, greasy cavern – a mechanic's magic cave, where Captain Smoothy-Smythe's loyal helpmates Slimey and Grimey O'Reilly do untold damage to people's cars at enormous expense.

The Captain is the owner and proprietor of the garage, but before going any further I need to give you a warning about him: he is not what he appears to be.

On first sight he seems a man of integrity and military bearing. In fact, he is a villain: a lying, deceitful, dangerous cheat. Don't be taken in by the fact that he has a neat moustache and wears smart check trousers and a blazer with bright brass buttons, or that he calls people 'old boy' or 'old bean' and says such things as 'jolly fine show'. He is a rotter, through and through.

So when the Captain read about the forthcoming Grand Prix with its five thousand pound first prize it set his criminal mind spinning.

A man like Captain Smoothy-Smythe could run the ABC Garage without even thinking about it. Simple little schemes like diluting the petrol with cheap paraffin, saying a car had been serviced when it hadn't, swopping good tyres for old ones and putting false new number plates on stolen cars and selling them, were second nature to him. He could do them in his sleep.

What the Captain needed was something really juicy to get his wicked teeth into – some scheme or wheeze that would bring in lots of lovely cash. He'd once had a go at running an Association for Bent Car Dealers, and he'd tried his hand at cheating at horse racing, but on both occasions he was discovered and foiled by Vera Pratt – you may have read about them.

This Grand Prix, however, with its beefy prize and a chance to defeat Vera Pratt, might be just what the Captain had been looking for!

He surveyed the front page once more: '*It would be splendid if the £5,000 first prize was won by someone in the local community,*' said Colonel Thundering-Blunderer, Chairman of the Grand Prix Committee.' 'Too jolly right, old bean!' said Captain Smoothy-Smythe to himself, and with a large grin on his face and a large gin in his hand, he put his feet up on his desk, stared at the grubby office ceiling, and started scheming!

While the Captain was thus engaged, Wally Pratt, Bean Pole, Ginger Tom and Bill Stickers were standing in a row in Morning Assembly at St Bernard's school.

Mr Edwards, aged forty-two, was addressing them on the matter of the Grand Prix: 'I'm sure you understand,' he said, 'that this is an opportunity for you children to be of service to others. All of you will be allocated duties at the race track, and I know that you will carry them out to the highest standards expected by St Bernard's, and that you will bring honour and credit to the school.'

Mr Edwards was a dignified man of medium build. He wore a neat grey suit and glasses and had thick ginger-brown hair which was always immaculately well-combed. His main interest in life was talking about pupils being either a credit or a disgrace to the school.

After Assembly Wally went with the note his mother had written and knocked on the Head's office door.

'Now then, what is it, young Pratt?' said Mr Edwards beckoning him in.

'I've got this note from my mum,' said Wally and he handed it over.

Mr Edwards read the note thoughtfully: 'I see . . . Your mother says she needs you in the sidecar on Saturday, and therefore asks if you can be let off official race track duties.'

He paused.

'I think in the circumstances it will be in order for me to comply with her request. After all, if you and your mother perform with honour it will bring credit to the school. It will be a welcome chance for you to show me what you can do, Wallace . . . I must say, young man, that I had it in mind to speak to you today anyway.'

Wally Pratt's heart sank and he looked at the floor. It was not the first time that Mr Edwards had spoken to him with this serious tone in his voice, and Wally knew that he was in for a longish lecture.

'I am far from satisfied with your standards and appearance, and with the general contribution you are making to the life of this school,' the Head continued. 'I feel, young man, that your performances at work and play are not up to scratch. At present, Pratt, you are as a weed growing in the garden of St Bernard's. You are a disgrace. Term ends a week today and I must warn you that unless by then you show that you have a lot more energy and initiative, and can act intelligently, your school report will bring you no credit, no credit at all!'

'Yes, Mr Edwards,' said Wally Pratt to the carpet, and he left the room.

3

The Captain Does Some Thinking

The more Captain Smoothy-Smythe thought about it, the more he liked the idea of entering the sidecar Grand Prix and winning it. All he'd need to do was get fixed up with a machine, find a passenger, and make sure that no one else could beat him.

He got up from behind his large cluttered desk and strode into the workshop at the back of the garage. 'I'll see what those pea-brained log-heads the O'Reilly brothers think about building me a bike,' he said to himself as he stepped over the remains of old cars that littered the blackened floor.

Slimey and Grimey O'Reilly were working in a distant corner of the room merrily removing the engine and chassis numbers from a Mini which the Captain had recently acquired from a man in a pub and that had had to be delivered to the garage after dark on the night before this story began.

'Ah! There you are, chaps! How's the work going?'

'Not too bad, Sir,' said Slimey O'Reilly. 'We've just got to make up a couple of nice new number plates and write out an MOT certificate, and she'll be ready for sale.'

'Well done, men!' said the Captain. He always spoke to the O'Reilly brothers as if they were soldiers under his command. 'I like to see you making sure that a vehicle is really well prepared before it's offered for sale: it's one of the most important principles of the motor trade . . . While I think of it, it might be an idea to spray the little blighter a new colour, just in case we get a visit from the boys in blue!'

'Very good, Sir,' said Grimey, wiping his hands on his filthy overalls.

'Before you do though, chaps, I'd greatly value your expert opinion on this sidecar race on Saturday. There's a hefty first prize, and I would like to win it. Do you think you could knock me up a really dashed fine motorbike and sidecar, in full racing nick, by the weekend? It would need to go like a rocket, of course. What do you think?'

'No problem, Sir,' said Grimey O'Reilly, putting the file he had been using behind his ear and standing upright. 'There's a very nice new Ferrari round the back waiting for a service. We could nick the engine out of it. That would give you all the power you'd need, and there's at least a couple of old motorbike and sidecar frames behind the oil tank.'

'It shouldn't take very long to weld something together for you, Gaffer – but it might not look too posh, mind,' warned his brother.

'Great stuff!' exclaimed the Captain. 'I don't know what I'd do without you chaps. Skilled, crooked mechanics like you are the backbone of our profession! Don't forget to finish the job on the Mini first – we can't win a sidecar Grand Prix if I'm sitting in the cop shop!'

'Don't worry, Sir!' said the O'Reilly brothers together, and they set to work on the poor little car with renewed vigour and brutality.

Captain Smoothy-Smythe went back to his office. 'So far so good,' he said to himself as he sat down once again at his desk. 'The next item on the agenda is a more tricky one . . . Where on earth am I going to find a passenger for the sidecar? It must be a pretty dangerous job sitting in a racing sidecar so I can't risk either of the O'Reillys: if one of them broke his thick neck my garage business would collapse instantly. What I need is an out-and-out idiot, a complete and utter half-wit, a twit, a moron who'd do anything for a small sum of money . . .' He drummed with his fingers on the desktop as he thought about it. 'Now, if only I knew a real thicko who'd be dim enough to do it . . .'

'Hallo, Guv!' said a voice at the door. The Captain looked up, and there stood Mr Dudley Cheque.

Captain Smoothy-Smythe is not a religious man, but the moment he heard Dud Cheque's voice he felt as if a prayer had been answered.

'Dud! My dear fellow! *How simply marvellous to see you again!*'

No one in their right mind would ever normally

say that it was simply marvellous to see Dud Cheque. He is a snivelling little man with dark mean eyes and a shifty way of walking that gives him the appearance of a rat with a hangover. However, the Captain had employed him on several previous criminal exploits, and he instantly sensed that he was about to do so again.

'Where have you been, old bean?' asked the Captain.

'Well, Guv, I've been in the jug again – after that time we tried to get away with Honest Bert's loot at the racecourse and I nicked the Bishop's false teeth and resprayed that racehorse.' (You may have read about this.) 'I only came out the day before yesterday. I wondered if you might have a job for me?'

'How amazing!' cried the Captain with a broad grin. 'It just so happens that I think I have – in fact I'm sure of it.'

Captain Smoothy-Smythe took a large bottle from the top drawer of his desk: 'Why don't you sit yourself down, make yourself comfortable, have a jolly old gin, and we'll talk about it.'

And that's exactly what they did.

4

That Friday

Before Wally Pratt left for school that Friday Vera checked on the state of his health:

'I hope you're looking after yourself, Wally. Are you eating well? I need you in tiptop condition for the race tomorrow. Here, take these to school in case you feel peckish.' She handed him a couple of large bars of chocolate.

'When school finishes come up to the race track and meet me at my pit. I'll be taking the bike up there after lunch and this evening there is time for testing and practising. The fastest practice laps will get pole position on the grid tomorrow.'

'Yes, Mum,' said Wally without a great deal of enthusiasm.

'Don't be late, mind – I need you in the sidecar when I make final adjustments and check out the handling characteristics.'

Then Bean Pole, Ginger Tom and Bill Stickers appeared at the front gate, and off they all went to school.

After Assembly Mr Edwards announced that the children in Wally's class were going to be on pit security duty and that he would be talking to them in groups during Break.

At fifteen minutes past eleven, therefore, the three boys were standing outside the Head's office.

'Right,' said Mr Edwards. 'As you three are such good friends of Wally Pratt I've decided to allocate you to the race pit that he and his mother will be using. St Bernard's is hoping they will win, and you will have the honour and privilege of helping them. Your job will be to keep an eye on their pit and pit lane area. You will be in charge of keeping it neat and tidy, and will assist the police in keeping un-authorized people out of it. As you will appreciate, this is a responsible task which needs to be done well. I am particularly concerned about your appearance – especially yours, Stukley – and I expect you to be well behaved, and well turned out, under-stand?'

'Yes, Mr Edwards,' they chorused.

'Good. The bikes are moving up to the track after lunch today, so you can have the afternoon off school in order to start your official duties. I shall be there this evening myself and will keep an eye out for you. Now good luck to you and of course to Mrs Pratt. Off you go.'

'Yes, Mr Edwards,' they chorused again, and left the room.

At the very same time as Mr Edwards was giving this briefing to three of his subordinates concerning the Grand Prix, Captain Smoothy-Smythe was doing the same thing to three of his.

Dud Cheque, Slimey O'Reilly and his brother were standing in a row in front of the Captain and his office desk.

'Now then, men,' he said. 'Before I officially inspect the machine which you two fine mechanics have prepared for me and my gallant sidecar passenger Dud Cheque' – he nodded towards Dud by way of acknowledgement – 'there are at least two items on the jolly old agenda that I need to discuss with you. It has always been part of my philosophy, men, that if I enter a race I always make absolutely sure that I win it! How do you think I do that, eh?'

He looked at them and waited for an answer.

'Dunno, Guv,' said Dud Cheque after an embarrassing pause during which the O'Reilly brothers wore their most gormless expressions.

'Think. Half-wits!' roared the Captain. Still nothing happened. 'What do you do if you want a racehorse to win a race?' asked the Captain speaking more quietly now but with menace in his voice. 'I'll tell you – *you nobble the others runners, of course!!*'

He leant forward with his knuckles down on the desk: 'You dope their food, or you bash their jockeys over the bonce with something blunt and heavy. Remember! Don't you numskulls have any grip of the basic principles of sportsmanship?!!'

The Captain stood upright and started to pace up and down like a General addressing men before a battle. He realized that if he was going to get the most out of his little army he would need to scare them: 'Let me make it clear that if I don't win tomorrow's race and the cash that goes with it, you lot will be out on your ears, understand? I expect you, from this moment onwards, to look for any and every opportunity to sabotage the opposition. *I want to see you showing enterprise, intelligence and initiative!* Get it?!'

'Yes,' they all mumbled, and started to shuffle towards the door.

'I haven't finished yet,' said the Captain, and they stopped: 'Any idiot with half a head could look at the form book for tomorrow's race and see where our main threat lies: Mrs Pratt. There's an Italian team with a good outfit, but they're like snails compared to her. I want that ghastly woman and her wobble-belly son fixed up for good and all. I've got a little something for each of us which may help.'

He opened the door of a metal safe that stood on the floor beside him and took out two pairs of long football socks. It was obvious that they were filled with something heavy. 'Do you know what these are for?' asked the Captain with a sneer.

'Playing football in, Sir,' replied Slimey O'Reilly, pleased to have got one of the Captain's questions right at last.

'NO, you *bumboil*!' roared the Captain. 'They're for socking people on the nut – that's why they're called socks! IDIOTS!! They are filled with damp sand. We conceal them about our persons, and the moment we get the chance we use them to cosh the ghastly Pratt woman, or her son, or for that matter any competitor who looks as if he might get between me and the five thousand quid first prize!! GET IT??!!'

Dud, Slimey and Grimey all agreed that they had more or less got it, and they took a sand-filled sock each and sidled back to the workshop.

'Bring the bike round the front for my inspection,' shouted the Captain to them as they went.

5

The O'Reilly Special

Captain Smoothy-Smythe strode out of his office and positioned himself on the garage forecourt. Though he was not a naturally nervous man his heart beat a little faster than usual as he waited for the O'Reilly brothers to show him the machine they had prepared for the next day's race: it was, after all, the key to winning a large sum of money.

He stood bolt upright with his hands behind his back – like a Grenadier Guard standing at ease. 'Come on, come on,' he muttered through his thin moustache.

Then he heard the double doors at the back of the garage being opened, and the next moment the midday air was split by a deafening, crackling roar – like the noise made by a low-flying jet. 'What the blazes?!' said the startled Captain out loud.

Then he saw it. Round the corner of the building came the Captain's very own motorbike and sidecar combination – the machine that would speed him to victory, glory, and five thousand pounds.

Slimey O'Reilly was driving it, with his brother sitting behind him. Dud Cheque was cowering in the sidecar.

'WHAT THE BALLY BLASTED BLAZES IS THAT?!!!' exclaimed the Captain as the machine came to a shuddering halt beside him.

'Isn't she a beauty, Sir?' said Slimey with a proud smile. 'It's an O'Reilly Special!' He turned off the engine to make conversation a little easier.

'I thought you blighters were building me a bike – *not a brass bedstead with multiple injuries!!*'

The Captain was saying this because the bike and sidecar that the O'Reillys had knocked up for him was not the sort of machine you might see on *Grandstand*. It was enormous, and looked as if it had been made mainly from scrap metal – which it had. It had cow-horn handlebars, a hooter, and six huge tractor exhaust pipes which stuck up in the air at the back. The sidecar seemed to consist of scaffolding, an old metal chair, wire, string, and the wheel of a pram. The whole thing had been sprayed black, which made it look sinister. It also made it look worse.

'It's not exactly *sleek*, is it?' remarked the Captain through gritted teeth.

'Well, we did warn you that it might not look posh,' replied Grimey O'Reilly. 'And anyway it's not looks that count. You should see it go!! It does nought to sixty before you can start a stop-watch, and the handling and aerodynamics are superb!'

'Aerodynamics?!' spluttered the Captain in disbelief. 'I've seen more aerodynamics on a milk-float!'

But he realized that shouting wasn't going to get him anywhere. This was the bike he was stuck with so he'd better work with it as best he could. He had a feeling deep inside that the sand-filled socks were going to play a more vital role in his race tactics than he had first envisaged.

'Right, men,' he said. 'I'll take you two' – he nodded towards the O'Reilly brothers – 'up to the track on the machine. You can teach me how to drive it. Cheque, you stay here and look after the petrol pumps for the afternoon, and join us at the track when you've locked up. By tonight, men, we'll put in a practice lap time that will take the world of motorcycle racing by storm!'

Dud got out of the sidecar and the O'Reillys rearranged themselves so that Captain Smoothy-Smythe could take the controls, with Slimey sitting behind him and Grimey in the chair. With a couple of kicks on the starter the Captain got the mighty engine going, and while Slimey shouted things in his ear like 'let out the clutch gently' the enormous and deadly looking contraption left the forecourt.

To be more precise: it set off in the direction of the local race track, doing wheelies down the road and swerving from verge to verge, with the startled Captain shouting things that are too rude for us to print here.

Dud Cheque, round-shouldered, shuffled into the pay kiosk at the front of the garage, and waited for customers. He sat there, bored, his hand inside his jacket idly fingering the sock full of sand that was hidden there.

The first customer to arrive was Mrs Vera Pratt.

She had spent the morning cleaning and polishing. She had washed her bike from handlebars to exhaust pipe, and had buffed up the sidecar nose cone and front fairings with a bright yellow duster until they shone in the midday sun. Unlike the outfit you have just been reading about, Vera's machine *did* look like something on *Grandstand*: it was magnificent. 'There,' she had said when she finished working on it. 'Any housewife could be proud of this bike.'

She had put a large empty petrol can into the sidecar, had taken her freshly-washed red leather racing suit from the airing cupboard, and her crash helmet from its hook, and had set off towards the ABC Garage to get enough fuel to see her through the practice sessions and the race itself.

'Fill her up, please,' said Vera to Dud Cheque as he sidled up to her. 'And fill this spare can as well. Four star, I want all the octane I can get!'

'OK, duck,' said Dud Cheque.

While Vera got the very last of her money from her purse – it was zipped into one of the pockets in her red racing suit – Dud filled the bike's tank, and started on the spare can as directed.

As he did so he pondered.

Now, Dud Cheque is not by nature a great thinker. In fact he's about as intelligent as a peanut butter sandwich, but he still had the Captain's words ringing in his ears about 'showing enterprise and initiative', and 'taking any and every opportunity to sabotage the opposition'.

He also had the sock filled with sand inside his jacket.

Dud could see, however, that Mrs Pratt was wearing a crash helmet, and it also dawned on him that even if she took it off and he sloshed her with the sock, he'd have a problem concealing the body for a whole twenty-four hours: someone would miss her.

So for the first and just about only time in his life Dud Cheque did something rather intelligent, something that even Captain Smoothy-Smythe might have approved of: it showed enterprise and initiative.

And I'm not going to tell you what it was.

6

Practice Laps

When school ended that day the warm summer sun was still pleasantly high in the sky. The birds sang, there was a soft breeze, and conditions at the track were perfect for fast practice lap times.

Mr Edwards got into his car to go there. He was excited at the prospect of some motor sport, and at the opportunity St Bernard's had been given to show what a fine school it was.

As he pulled out of the school gates he saw Wally on the pavement.

'Come on, hop in, young Pratt. I'm on my way to the track – I expect your mother will be waiting for you.'

'Thanks,' said Wally, and he got into the car.

'Don't forget what I told you, Wallace, I'm looking at your behaviour very carefully, and I'm expecting to see an improvement in your standards of appearance, energy and initiative.'

'Yes, Mr Edwards,' said Wally Pratt.

When they got to the race track it was buzzing

with activity. Brightly coloured lorries and trailers were distributed across the paddocks and car parks, gleaming machines purred round the track with the sunlight flashing from time to time as it reflected on their Perspex windshields and highly polished sides. There were marquees and tents, and flags and bunting. It reminded the Headteacher of a tournament scene from a nursery history book.

He smiled at the thought and, while Wally headed for the pits, Mr Edwards strolled towards the car parks where some of the girls from 4 A were helping to put up ropes with small triangles of red plastic on them to form lanes.

The pits were a long line of low buildings rather like a block of garages. They stood on a pit lane that looped off the main track, and had enough space at the front of it for mechanics to work on racing cars or bikes.

There had been a bustle of activity at the pits all afternoon. Captain Smoothy-Smythe had, by this time, mastered the basics of propelling the O'Reilly Special round the track. He had completed several circuits fairly successfully with Grimey in the sidecar, and the brothers were now attending to a few minor adjustments – tightening a piece of wire here, thumping something with a hammer there.

Next to the Captain's pit on one side was the crack Italian team. Michele and Marco Carburetti were, like the O'Reillys, brothers. They were not like the O'Reillys in any other respect. Their

machine was the smartest, sleekest, smoothest thing the Captain, or anyone else at the track that day, had ever seen.

It was green and orange, the colours of the Italian flag, and had the grace and poise of a leaping cheetah, and the Carburetti brothers wore skin-tight designer leather overalls in colours that

7

What the Captain Was Up To

What happened was this: Captain Smoothy-Smythe, having got the hang of the O'Reilly Special, decided to go for a short walk. The brothers were doing some work on the bike and sidecar, and there didn't seem much point in doing any more practising until Dud Cheque arrived from the garage and could sit in the sidecar.

The Captain realized that he had thrown down a gauntlet to his men – he had threatened them with the sack if they didn't show initiative and look for opportunities to nobble the opposition, especially Mrs Pratt.

Captain Smoothy-Smythe, as a natural leader of men – especially criminals – knew that it is important to set a good example.

If a little stroll round the race track should lead to the chance of doing something or other that would drastically diminish the chances of another team's success, it would show that the Captain was prepared to work just as hard as his men. It would show

'Well, he's got plenty of it to throw,' remarked Bean Pole, and they all laughed.

It was rather a pity that at that moment they weren't attending properly to their official race track duties. You will remember that they were supposed to be responsible for Mrs Pratt's pit, its tidiness and security.

If they had been more attentive, and had not been so spellbound by Wally and his ton-up mum, they might have seen what Captain Smoothy-Smythe was up to!

that Captain Smoothy-Smythe led 'from the front'.

With his hands behind his back he walked casually down the front of the pits.

The first one he came to belonged to the Carburetti brothers. They were obviously well pleased with the practice times they had already achieved, because Marco was standing in the middle of the pit

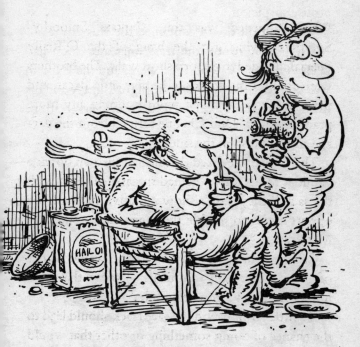

garage blow-drying Michele's hair. Their amazing bike was parked in full view on the pit forecourt with lots of people taking photos of it: there was nothing imaginative that the Captain could do there.

He had walked by the Pratt pit at the time when Wally was putting on his helmet. He had seen that the ghastly Mrs Pratt, as he called her, was about to go out on the track, but as there were kids all over the place the Captain walked on past, anxious not to arouse suspicion.

The next pit down contained the Russian team. Many people round the track that afternoon had been saying how good they were, and the Captain was keen to get a look at them. Igor Blimey and his team-mate Tumbleoff were deep in conversation.

'Probably discussing tactics,' mumbled the Captain to himself. 'Anyway, I'm not going to rush in and scupper their bike in a hurry – I don't want the might of the jolly old Soviet Union descending on me. What good would five thousand quid be if I'm sitting in a Siberian labour camp?' The very thought of it sent a shudder up the back of his blazer.

The Captain found that in all the pits there were too many people and too much activity for him to get close enough to do any damage. He realized that he'd just have to wait: his moment would come.

Actually his moment came very soon because when he was walking back to his own pit, past Mrs Pratt's again, the situation there had changed.

She and her son were obviously out on practice, and the three scruffy kids who had earlier been standing in the garage were now out on the grass gazing at the bikes coming round the track. They had their backs to the pit.

Captain Smoothy-Smythe stepped through the pit doorway as fast as a ferret down a rabbit hole: one moment he was visible, the next he had gone.

Once inside, his sharp, keen eyes surveyed the dark interior of the garage, like a burglar looking for the family silver.

He went to the back wall and instantly saw something that made his heart sing: there by the door to her storeroom stood a spare can of petrol!

–

The Captain spoke out loud to himself: 'The old girl obviously plans to use this for refuelling tomorrow – she'll have a job if it's empty!'

All the pit garages had back doors which opened out into a small drivers' paddock. It only took the Captain a minute or two to pick up Vera's spare can of petrol, nip out through the back door, nip in

again through *his* back door, pour the contents of the can into the tank of his mighty O'Reilly Special, and return the empty container to Mrs Pratt's garage.

As I pointed out in the last chapter, if Bean Pole, Ginger Tom and Bill Stickers had been keeping an eye on Mrs Pratt's pit they would have seen him; but they weren't, so they didn't.

When the Captain finally returned to his own pit area he was pleased with himself: he had a broad smile on his face and a spring in his step and a general feeling of well-being that came from the thought that he had just taken one step nearer five thousand pounds.

Dud Cheque arrived.

'Ah, there you are, Cheque, old man. Get your helmet on and I'll show you round the jolly old track. Riding in the sidecar is a piece of cake! You'll love it, old bean!'

'Rightchooare, Guv,' said Dud Cheque, and the Captain couldn't help noticing that there was a broad smile on *his* face too!

'What the dickens are you so jolly chuffed about, Cheque?' asked the Captain, intrigued.

'Oh . . . I'll tell you later, Guv,' said Dud as he pulled his crash helmet on.

Slimey O'Reilly gave the bike a friendly pat on the saddle: 'There you are, Sir. She's all ready to go.'

And the Captain took his place once more on the mighty bike with Dud crouched in the sidecar.

'*TIMED PRACTICE LAPS WILL STOP IN TEN MINUTES*' said the race track loudspeakers.

'What does that mean, Guv?' asked Dud.

'It means, old fruit, that we've only got ten more minutes in which to do a really fast lap: the bikes with the best times tonight will start at the front of the grid tomorrow. It's essential, Cheque, that we do well, so hold tight and lean out when I yell at you, got it?'

Dud said that he had got it and off they went.

The Captain took it fairly easy on the first lap and hardly did any wheelies at all.

Ginger Tom, Bean Pole and Bill Stickers were quite impressed when they first saw the O'Reilly Special.

'Cor, look at that monster!' said Bean Pole. 'And what a racket!!'

They could instantly see however that Dud Cheque had none of Wally's ability or agility in a sidecar. The Captain spotted it too:

'Lean out, Cheque, you half-wit!' he shouted above the din of engine. 'Don't just sit there like a constipated pensioner!'

'I don't feel safe, Guv,' yelled Dud.

'You're not here to feel *safe*, Cheque, you're here

to help me win five thousand quid, now LEAN OUT! If Old Ma Pratt's ghastly child can do it so can you.'

'Oh, I shouldn't worry about the Pratts if I were you, Guv,' shouted Dud as they swung into the long back straight. 'You see, that's why I was smiling, I've fixed her good and proper, just like you asked. You're going to be really pleased when you hear what I've done.'

'What *have* you done?' asked the Captain, slowing down a little so that he could hear better.

'I've shown initiative, Guv. Mrs Pratt came to the garage, see, and asked me to fill up a spare can of petrol – she'll be using it for the race tomorrow. I didn't just put petrol in it, Guv, *I emptied all the sand from my sand-filled sock into it! A couple of laps and her engine will clog up for good and all! Sand ruins an engine in no time!*'

At that moment the O'Reilly Special's engine gave a cough, and with a chug and a bang it slowed to walking pace. Then with a final splutter it died altogether.

8

Mechanical Failure

'CHEQUE! YOU HALF-BAKED BELLY-BUTTON BUMBOIL! *DUMBO!! I've a good mind to tear you to pieces and spread your remains all over this rotten, stinking, blooming tarmac! PINHEAD!!'*

'What have I done, Guv?' said Dud. This wasn't the reaction he'd been expecting.

'*DONE??!!*' roared the Captain. 'You've scuppered my chances of winning a small fortune, you've written off a perfectly good Ferrari engine, and you've handed victory to Mrs Ghastly Pratt on a plate! *That's what you've done! PEA-WITTED OAF!!*'

The Captain leaped off the dead motorbike and stood on the grass verge shaking his fists. I say stood, but actually he was jumping up and down.

'How do you mean?' said Dud. 'You told us to nobble the opposition and that's what I did. Mrs Pratt won't win a race with a sock load of sand in her fuel tank, Guv!'

'She hasn't got a sock load of sand in *her* fuel tank,

BUM-ACHE! WE HAVE! *I had the intelligence to pinch her petrol!!*'

'Well, how was I to know you'd go and do that?' asked Dud Cheque. He thought it was a reasonable question in the circumstances.

'DON'T SPLIT HAIRS AND GET ALL TECHNICAL WITH ME, CHEQUE,' bellowed the Captain. '*I'M GOING TO BEAT YOU TO DEATH!*'

Captain Smoothy-Smythe looked round for something to beat Dud Cheque to death with. He couldn't see anything suitable so he went to rip one of the large exhaust pipes off the O'Reilly Special to use as a weapon. It was scalding hot and the Captain leaped into the air the moment his fingers touched it.

'GGRRRRR!!!!' he shouted in agony. 'Cheque! If you and those spud-faced mechanics don't put this matter right, you won't just be out on your ears – you'll be taken apart and chopped up into bite-sized chunks and scattered all the way from Silverstone to Brands Hatch!! *GET IT??!!!!!*'

Once more Dud Cheque had to agree that he had got it, and he climbed off the sidecar and slunk back towards the pits to discuss the problem with the O'Reilly brothers.

Captain Smoothy-Smythe sat down on the grass. He is not the sort of man who cries easily, but I wouldn't have been surprised if a tiny tear rolled down his red cheek and disappeared into his revolting moustache.

Then he got up, said something very rude, kicked the O'Reilly Special, and pushed it over the grass and into a ditch where its ruined engine and glowing exhausts sunk with a steamy hiss into a pool of filthy black water.

As he did so, Vera and Wally sped past on their machine, but they didn't see him. Both of them were far too busy attempting the fastest lap of the afternoon. Vera's face behind her visor wore an expression of sheer determination – with gritted teeth and eyes fixed on the road ahead. Wally threw himself from side to side like something in a fun-fair. One moment he was draped across the pillion behind his mother's leather-clad backside, the next he dangled a centimetre or two from the flesh-tearing surface of the track, way out beyond the sidecar wheel.

'That's the way, Wally!' shouted his mother encouragingly from the bike. 'Give it some wellie!'

Wally gave it some wellie till his teeth chattered.

With Vera's driving skill and Wally's ample weight redistributing itself to perfection there was no doubt that they were doing well, and putting up a very fast time.

About half a lap ahead of them another team was

also doing well. The Italian outfit slinked and snaked round the track like a string of oiled spaghetti. They took every turn and curve with a silky rhythm that was admired by all who saw it. Everyone agreed that the Carburetti brothers were a great team, and their bike was a world beater.

At ten past six the paddock behind the pits was

filled with riders and passengers and their fans. All eyes were fixed on the large electronic scoreboard and lap counter, and breaths were held as the practice lap times and consequent grid positions for the next day's start were flashed up.

The Italians were first: they had pole position. Behind them by only a few seconds was Vera, closely followed by the Russians, and a Brazilian team led by a driver called Ayrton Sennapod. Then there was a whole cluster of teams from various towns and countries.

At the bottom of the scoreboard there was a special notice:

NOTE: BECAUSE OF MECHANICAL FAILURE CAPTAIN SMOOTHY-SMYTHE'S ABC GARAGE TEAM HAS WITHDRAWN AND WILL NOT RACE.

'Don't be too sure about that, old bean!' said the Captain through gritted teeth as he strode home across the back of the paddock.

9

The Night Before Race Day

Everyone's brain has a mind of its own. This fact is
well illustrated by the way that later that night all
the characters in this story were having their own
different and individual thoughts and dreams.

Down in his tidy house opposite the school gates,
Mr Edwards, the forty-two-year-old Headteacher,
was tucked up in bed in his pyjamas. His teeth were
well brushed and his hair was as immaculately
combed as usual, but the inside of his head was a
whirl with unruly dreams about tomorrow's race.
One moment terrible things happened that brought
disgrace and shame to him and his school, the next
he was a triumphant hero – with a wreath of laurel
leaves round his shoulders, spraying the crowd with
a shower of champagne from a huge bottle.

In another part of town, in a room that would
make your bedroom look like an advert for a top
hotel, lay Dud Cheque.

He was huddled under an old coat with a muffler
round his neck and a cloth cap on his head because of

the draught that came in through a broken pane of glass in the window.

His wild and dreadful dreams dwelt on only one topic – being beaten to death, chopped into chunks, and spread all over a race track. To make matters worse the Captain of his dreams then jumped up and down all over his remains.

Dud woke with a start, but realizing that it was only a nightmare he rolled over, wiped his long damp nose on the grey muffler, and went back to sleep.

Wally Pratt dreamed bone-shaking dreams which as well as containing a lot of sidecar racing also included a large green monster that bore a strange resemblance to Mr Edwards.

In the bedroom next door to him Vera Pratt snored lightly and dreamed dreams of victory. Her magnificent machine was drawn by six Lloyds Bank black horses on a lap of honour over a race-track surfaced with ten pound notes! She was inter-viewed for television by the most beautiful man she had ever seen, and his final question was 'Vera Pratt . . . Will you marry me?' An elaborate wedding followed, with her dressed from head to toe in snow-white racing leathers, a broad lace train bil-lowing down from the back of a new diamond encrusted full-face crash helmet with tinted glass veil.

Captain Smoothy-Smythe, in stark contrast to everyone else I've told you about, lay wide awake. He stared at his bedroom's moonlit ceiling, and schemed.

The more his criminal brain thought about it, the more he realized that if he was going to salvage anything from the situation, he would have to work with and through his men. Scaring them witless was all very well, and highly necessary with a man like Dud Cheque who was about as useless as a whippet with a wooden leg, but tact and diplomacy were needed too. 'After all,' the Captain thought, 'I do *need* Dud Cheque . . . if I can somehow or other get back into the race I need him in the sidecar. He's indispensable: he's the only man I know whose neck could get broken in fifteen places and it wouldn't matter a hoot to me.'

By the time that pale sunbeams lit the undersides of high clouds in the eastern sky, and the birds started twittering in the gutters outside his room, the Captain had hatched a battle campaign that might – just might – give him the victory and the five thousand pounds that he so passionately craved.

'Right!' he said to himself as he dressed and brushed a speck or two of dandruff from the collar of his well-cut blazer. 'It will need teamwork, and good luck, but fortune favours the jolly old brave, as they say, and it's certainly worth a bash. I shall address the troops the moment I get to the track, and we'll put my plan of attack into action immediately!'

10

The Captain's Plan

'THIS IS THE PITS!' said Captain Smoothy-Smythe.

'We know that, Chief,' said Slimey O'Reilly.

'Not *that* sort of pits, numskull – the pits, the *absolute* pits, the worst position we could be in.' He straightened his back in order to tower above the three men in front of him. Then he looked them straight in the eye:

'In my time, men, I've been in some pretty sticky situations. I've been beaten about the moustache with an adjustable spanner by mad Madam Pratt, I've been rugger tackled by her revolting son and his chums, and I've tried to win a horse race with a three-legged racehorse; but never in my whole life have I appeared on the morning of a Motorbike and Sidecar Grand Prix and tried to win it without a motorbike or, for that matter, *a stinking rotten side-car*!!' The Captain's face started to go red: he was certainly winning the attention of his troops.

'All, however, is not lost. With some constructive

teamwork, and working under my guidance and leadership, there may still be a way to win through.' He paused for a moment, then continued: 'I would like to point out though, chaps, that if any of you should happen to muck up the plan I am about to reveal to you even in the slightest, it will be necessary for me to break your stupid spines into handy sized pieces and skin you alive over a hot fire. Get it?'

'Yes,' mumbled Dud and Grimey and Slimey O'Reilly, more or less in unison.

'Good. I thought it only fair to point that out before we start. Right then, the plan I have hatched is, like all great military schemes, simple, yet daring. It consists of a two-pronged attack – an attack, as we used to say in the army, on two battle fronts.'

You don't need me to tell you that the Captain had never actually been in the army.

'We therefore need to split into two teams, or patrols, each with a specific task. Patrol A will be me and Slimey here, and Patrol B is made up of you two.' He nodded towards Dud Cheque and Grimey O'Reilly.

'Here is what we do. It will not have escaped your notice that our Italian friends, in the pit next door, not only have pole position on the grid this afternoon, they also have the fastest thing on three wheels since Concorde – and some jolly flashy racing clothes to go with it. Patrol A, that's me and Slimey here, will go next door, bop them on the nut with something blunt and heavy, and capture their designer race suits and helmets. This afternoon Dud and I will ride their bike instead of them. With all their trendy kit on no one will spot the difference, even when we go up and pocket the prize money! OK?'

'That's brilliant, Sir!' said Slimey, full of admiration.

'Yes, it is,' replied the Captain. 'But any military strategist like me can see that there is still a flaw in it – it's not foolproof because of one thing . . .' He paused just in case any of his men could see what it was, but as none of them could, he continued: 'The problem is that though the Italian machine is absolutely world class, it has to start the race with Mrs Pratt in second place on the grid. With a fanatic racer like her looking up your exhaust pipe all afternoon you can't ever be certain of victory. Patrol B therefore will have the job of immobilizing, for once and for all, Mrs Ghastly Pratt and her revolting wobble-belly son.'

He looked directly at Dud Cheque. '*No action you take can be too drastic or deadly to finish her off.* Do you understand me, Cheque?'

'Yes, Guv,' said Dud Cheque.

'Good – because the leadership of Patrol B, Cheque, is the last chance you'll get to save your miserable, stinking little skin! Fail me and I'll remove it inch by square inch and hang you out to dry from the top of the garage flagpole. OK, buddy boy?!'

'OK, Guv,' said Dud.

'Right,' snarled the Captain. 'Let's get on with it!'

11

The First Prong

Mr Edwards was also at the Grand Prix race track in good time that Saturday morning. He knew it was his duty to see that all the pupils of St Bernard's school were performing well.

He walked across the paddock behind the pits, and was particularly pleased to see Bean Pole, Ginger Tom and Bill Stickers all heading in the direction of the pits.

'Good morning, boys,' he said. 'I hope you're all prepared for a good solid day's work – I'm sure Mrs Pratt will be looking to you to give her pit a first-class service.'

'Yes, Mr Edwards,' said the boys.

'Be vigilant and attentive at all times: regrettably events like this race sometimes attract a criminal element, and unscrupulous deeds may be done. Watch out – I shall give you all the support I can; after all, the honour of St Bernard's is at stake.'

'Yes, Mr Edwards,' said the boys again, and off they went to find Wally and his mum.

Vera and Wally were already in their pit garage. Wally was watching his mother at work. She was going over the engine and front forks with a feather duster, whistling while she worked:

'Wally, don't just stand there – bring me a torque wrench and socket set from the store-room, I want to check the geometry on the sidecar. I think it's still tracking to the left at speed.'

'You what, Mum?'

'Just bring me my tools – there's a good lad, I haven't got time to explain. Honestly, a woman's work is never done!'

Wally went to the store and unlocked it and carried his mother's tool kit to the side of the bike. It weighed a ton.

'The nose of the sidecar took a few knocks yesterday, Wally,' she said. 'Get the red aerosol and spray where the paint is chipped – I want it to look its best for this afternoon.'

Wally did as his mother asked, and was sitting on the floor happily zapping the marks on the gleaming red sidecar when Bean Pole and the others arrived.

'Good morning, you horrors,' said Vera to them cheerily. 'How are you?'

'Fine thank you, Mrs Pratt,' said Bean Pole. Wally's friends liked his mother, but they were slightly in awe of her: she was nothing like their mothers, and that made her difficult to get used to.

'We've just seen old Edwards,' said Bill Stickers. 'He says we've got to keep a really good eye on the pit today because of "criminal elements".'

'So here we are,' explained Ginger Tom.

'Good,' said Vera Pratt.

The boys watched in admiration as she adjusted bolts on the sidecar couplings. Wally finished with the red spray and stood up.

'Make yourself useful, Wally. Get that petrol can from the back of the garage and fill the tank.'

Wally went obediently to the back of the garage.

Vera Pratt was wearing a black leather jacket over

her racing suit with 'Housewives Rule OK' on the back of it in brass studs. What Wally said next sent a small shudder up the back of it.

'This can is empty, Mum!'

'I don't like this at all!' said Vera, a determined look coming over her face. 'Someone's pinched our petrol!' She looked straight at Wally and his friends. 'Right, you boys – you are going to have to be on the look-out all right. The lost petrol doesn't matter – thank heavens we've discovered it early enough and I have time to replace it, but it means that your Headteacher may be right: someone round here is up to no good! Watch out for dirty work!'

She gritted her teeth and got on with polishing the handlebars with a bright yellow duster.

In the pit next door to Vera's, Michele and Marco Carburetti were having a discussion. They were having it in Italian so there's no point in me writing it down. Roughly translated they were saying that they thought it was time that they went out and did a few warm-up laps.

They had already pulled on their very slinky orange and green all-in-one suits. Michele was putting on some aftershave and Marco was making final adjustments to his hair-do before putting on his helmet, when Patrol A, consisting of Captain Smoothy-Smythe and Slimey O'Reilly, entered through the back door of the pit garage.

A moment later a sock full of sand, expertly brandished by the Captain, descended on Michele's skull. 'MAMMA MIA!! ME NUTTO!!' he shrieked as he sank to the garage floor.

'OH NO!! ME HAIR-DO – EES-A RUINED!!' added Marco as he received similar treatment at the hand of Slimey O'Reilly.

After a considerable struggle the Captain and Slimey managed to get the two unconscious Italians out of their skin-tight racing suits.

'Jolly good work,' said the Captain approvingly. 'Now let's lock them in their own store-room at the back here, and the moment Cheque is ready he and I will put on these suits and go out and get the hang of this amazing machine.'

The sleek Italian bike and sidecar stood in the centre of the garage: it looked almost menacingly beautiful.

Slimey and he then dragged the poor Carburettis, dressed only in their designer boxer shorts, to the back of the pit garage and locked them in the store.

Before leaving by the back door the Captain turned and surveyed the bike with a look of triumph on his face.

The first prong of his two-pronged attack had worked like a dream!

12

The Second Prong

Mr Edwards had a very enjoyable morning. He did several tours of inspection and on every occasion when he came across pupils from St Bernard's they seemed to be doing a good job.

The car-park helpers were ensuring that cars were parked in neat and orderly rows, children on litter duty were keeping the place spotless, and the pits area appeared orderly and efficient.

Mr Edwards was a man who liked things to look right: 'everything in the right place' was one of his favourite mottoes, and tidiness and order were his watchwords.

He walked to the top of the pit paddock and surveyed the scene. The sky was pleasantly blue, with only the occasional puffy white cloud to untidy it. The breeze was cooling, the birds were singing happily, and the race ground looked spruce and shipshape. Mr Edwards regarded it as all very satisfactory.

He was a little surprised therefore when he saw

two men bundle Wally Pratt through the back door of one of the pits.

As you may have guessed, the two men belonged to Patrol B.

What had happened was this. Wally had finished the retouching job on his mum's bike and sidecar. He'd got ready for the race, and then had hung around for an hour or so while his mum made final adjustments to this and that. He had got bored. Bean Pole and the others were busy on pit duty, so Wally picked up his crash helmet and decided to go for a stroll.

He was innocently walking along minding his own business, and had just passed the open back door of a pit a couple down from his mum's, when two men emerged from it and grabbed him from behind.

'*Make a fuss and I'll break yer arm!*' Dud Cheque hissed in Wally's left ear.

'Me too,' said Grimey in the right one.

They forced Wally's arms up behind his back, turned him round and bundled him through the back door of the garage. In a trice Grimey had a gag round Wally's mouth and a rope round his wrists and ankles. He was pushed without ceremony into the store-room; the key turned in the lock with a sickening clunk.

Dud Cheque, leader of patrol B, was pleased with

the swift efficiency of the daring kidnap. He thought it had shown great initiative and opportunism, and he felt sure that it had been carried out so suddenly and quickly that no one could have seen it.

As so often happens with Dud Cheque, he was wrong.

Mr Edwards at the back of the paddock could hardly believe his eyes. Had he really just witnessed one of his pupils being manhandled and kidnapped? Wally Pratt was by no means one of the jewels in the crown of St Bernard's: he was not Mr Edward's idea of a star pupil, far from it, but the Headteacher was a man of principle. It was his duty to protect his children however revolting they might be. (I expect your Headteacher thinks the same.)

Mr Edwards was across that field before you could say 'Dinner Lady'.

The back door of the pit was just closing as he arrived at it. He stuck his foot in it to keep it open, and banged loudly at it, shouting as he did so: 'Excuse me a moment – *you've got one of my pupils in there!!*'

Dud and Grimey opened the door a little, and Mr Edwards wagged his finger at them:

'Don't think I didn't see what you did just now, and don't think you can get away with it! You've got young Pratt in there against his will. Release him this instant – you are no credit to your profession – in fact *YOU ARE A DISGRACE*!'

'Oh, we are, are we?!' said Dud Cheque with a horrible smirk. As he said it Grimey O'Reilly went into action.

He charged from the dark depths of the pit garage and butted the amazed Headteacher in the middle of his stomach. 'AHHHHH!' yelled Mr Edwards – and he doubled up forwards at the impact.

As the top of the Headteacher's skull presented itself to him Dud Cheque acted impulsively and stupidly. With the speed of a striking cobra Dud's hand shot inside his jacket and brought out his football sock cosh.

With a swish he brought it down on the Head's noble dome.

You will not have failed to realize that the sock had no sand in it, its contents having been emptied into Vera Pratt's petrol can the day before. Instead of the Headteacher falling to the ground with a crash, unconscious, and being swept up into the garage out of harm's way – which is what Dud meant to happen – the sock did little damage.

That is not to say, however, that it caused nothing to happen.

Something did happen which, to Mr Edwards, was far worse than being clubbed unconscious: the glancing blow from the empty sock hit him on the top of his well-combed hair and it fell off, in one piece.

It was a wig, and when Mr Edwards straightened up, he was as bald as a billiard ball.

13

Mission Accomplished!

The Headteacher went to pick the wig up, but Dud Cheque put his foot on it. Mr Edwards did the only thing he could do in the circumstances: he fled.

Dud bent down and looked at the furry mat of ginger-brown hair. It was no longer immaculately combed. It looked more like a rat that had been run over by a bus. Dud kicked it behind the back door: he couldn't see the owner of the wig making any more fuss – Dud is not a clever creature, but he knows that people who wear wigs don't like other people to know about it.

'He'll lie low, whoever he was!' he said to Grimey, who nodded in agreement.

A moment later Captain Smoothy-Smythe and Slimey O'Reilly entered the pit through the front doors:

'Right then, Cheque – the race will begin any minute, let's have your report from Patrol B!'

'We did pretty well, Guv. We've kidnapped the Pratt kid! We've got him locked in the store-room. I can't see Mrs Pratt even entering the race now – not without a passenger!'

'I say, Cheque,' said the Captain, a broad beaming smile spreading across his unpleasant face, 'for once in your life you seem to have done something intelligent! Very good. Well done, old bean, mission accomplished! Once this race is run and won, you and I might go and have a jolly old knees up! I'll buy you a gin or two!'

The Captain hardly ever spoke to Dud Cheque like this: it sent a warm glow through his horrible little frame.

'We, too, have triumphed,' continued the Captain. 'Here, put this on.'

He handed Dud one of the Italian racing suits which Slimey was carrying. 'It may not be a great fit, but once we're into them and have these flashy helmets on no one will be able to tell that we're not the real thing! Hurry, Cheque, I've got to get the hang of their bike before the official warm-up lap which starts the race.'

Dud Cheque and Captain Smoothy-Smythe stripped down to their underpants. It was not a pretty sight – I advise you to look the other way.

Slimey and Grimey stood beside them like armour bearers, holding out all the Italian race gear, the suits, helmets, boots and gloves.

'I say,' said the Captain. 'How the heck do those fellows get into this stuff?'

The problem was that the Carburetti brothers were built like natural athletes. They were both of medium build, and very nicely proportioned with a pleasant coating of muscles in all the right places.

Captain Smoothy-Smythe, on the other hand, was tall and skinny, with very long legs. The designer racing suit had not been designed with him in mind. It was far, far too small and tight. Getting his feet and legs down the trouser part of the all-in-one was hard enough, but when it came to trying to squeeze his trunk and arms into the top half the trouble really started:

'Come on, Slimey, pull the thing up over my back! Get my shoulders in!'

'Have you got a shoe-horn, Sir?' asked Slimey O'Reilly innocently.

'Don't be daft, man!' snarled the Captain. 'There's five thousand quid at stake!'

Dud Cheque was much smaller and punier than Marco Carburetti, whose suit he was getting into. The legs were therefore all corrugated round his knees, and the arms came down and almost covered his gloves.

The whole thing had the wrinkled and creased look of the top of a cold rice pudding.

'Do you think you might grow into it?' asked Grimey O'Reilly.

'Stop messing about!' hissed the Captain to him. 'And let's get next door and get their machine started. Are you sure young Pratt is secure – he seems to be very quiet, doesn't he?'

'He'll be OK,' said Grimey.

'Good, come on then. We'll go round through the back doors.'

Captain Smoothy-Smythe and Dud Cheque, disguised as Italian masters of the art of motorcycle racing, nipped out into the paddock and back in through the back door of the Carburetti pit.

As they went they heard an announcement on the track loudspeaker system: *'All competing teams to the start grid, please. Official warm-up lap starts in five minutes.'*

14

A New Experience for Mr Edwards

Does your teacher wear a wig?

How do you know?

When Mr Edwards, Headteacher of St Bernard's school, lost his wig, it was probably the worst moment in his life.

What was he to do? The racetrack and grounds were full of children from his school, which made him want to bury himself somewhere and never be seen again, and yet he had evidence that there was dirty work going on, with one of his pupils having been snatched in front of his very own eyes!

He had no time to think it over: he had to act immediately, and he did. Now the whole school was on trial; its honour was at stake.

He had to swallow his pride and put St Bernard's first. He would go straight away to Mrs Pratt and inform her of the danger he feared her son was in.

It was not a very difficult course of action to follow, because by the time he decided on it he had travelled the short distance from the back door of the ABC Garage pit to the back door of Mrs Pratt's.

He dashed in through it; with luck no pupils would have seen him and he could hide in the pit and go home after dark without being spotted. He was sure Mrs Pratt would keep his secret, especially as he might be saving her son's life.

His heart sank the moment he was through the door. Mrs Pratt was at the front of the pit, and she was talking to Bean Pole, Ginger Tom and Bill Stickers.

He was brave: 'Mrs Pratt?' he said.

She and the three pupils turned round. Their mouths opened in amazement as the truth struck them: it was Mr Edwards without any hair!

'Mrs Pratt, you can see that I am in an embarrassing situation. However, I had to come to tell you about Wallace.'

'Where on earth *is* he!' exclaimed Vera with panic in her voice. 'I need him here, now, in the sidecar! *The race starts in five minutes!!*'

'I greatly fear that he has been kidnapped. I saw him being dragged into the pit two doors up from here. It was there that I had the misfortune to lose my special "Look-Ten-Years-Younger" hairpiece.'

His voice had an empty howling sound in it.

Vera's face flushed with rage: 'It's that crew from the ABC Garage! I knew there was dirty work afoot. *I bet it was them who pinched my petrol!* Typical!!'

'We must rescue him!' exclaimed the Headteacher, remembering his duty.

'We can't do that!' shrieked Vera Pratt. 'I've got to win the Grand Prix first. Bean Pole and the boys can go looking for Wally.' She nodded towards them. '*The problem is that now I haven't got a sidecar passenger*!'

Vera Pratt looked thoughtful. She stood there in

her red racing leathers, her hand over her chin, and a frown on her forehead.

'OFFICIAL WARM-UP LAP STARTS IN THREE MINUTES. THREE MINUTES PLEASE!'

'GOT IT!' exclaimed Vera. 'I've got it! Come on, Baldilocks, *into the sidecar!'*

Mr Edwards could not believe his ears.

'What are you talking about, Mrs Pratt? I've never even been in a sidecar in my life.'

'Oh, I'll teach you the basics on the warm-up lap, and you'll soon get the idea. I taught a Bishop how to do it once, it was a doddle! Anyway,' she added, 'the honour of your school is at stake. If we do well it will bring credit to St Bernard's!'

This point struck home with the Headteacher: perhaps she was right. Perhaps it was his duty to assist her.

'But I haven't got any of that tight clothing you all wear,' he said, realizing that he was dressed in his best grey suit.

'Oh, don't worry about all that – it's just for show. Get in.'

'TWO MINUTES TO GO! ALL TEAMS TO THE STARTING GRID IMMEDI-ATELY!'

Mr Edwards swallowed hard. Then he climbed into the sidecar: it was like a bad dream.

Vera Pratt pulled on her gloves and helmet and with a deft kick she started the mighty engine. It roared into life with a snarl and a swirl of smoke.

Mr Edwards was thinking about the awful fact that a vast crowd was going to see his bald head, when a thought struck him: 'Hang on, Mrs Pratt! I haven't got a crash helmet!'

'I'll fix that,' said Vera and she leaped off the bike again.

She picked up the red aerosol that Wally had been using that morning, and with three sharp squirts she sprayed his bald head red. Then she peeled a plastic sticker off the side of the bike that said 'KESTREL GTX *best oil in the world*' and stuck it on the side of his head.

'There,' she said. 'No one will notice.'

And off they sped down the pit lane and into second position on the Grand Prix starting grid.

15

They're Off!

'THREE!'
  'TWO!'
  'ONE!'
  'THEY'RE *OFF!!* This is Slury Talker for the BBC at the Motorbike and Sidecar Grand Prix, and they're all off to an *amazing* start! The sound is *deafening*! Into the first bend and it's the Italians in the lead with Tumble off the Russian and Sennapod and the local team Mrs Pratt all in hot pursuit! This is *so* exciting!'

It was indeed exciting. Captain Smoothy-Smythe found it so, and he soon forgot the discomfort of the Italian designed leather racing suit. With eyes narrowed on the road ahead and chin and jaw jutting out with determination, he opened the throttle on the sleek Italian bike and crouched low as it sprang from bend to straight like a leaping tiger.

Vera Pratt was in similar mood. Side by side with Igor Blimey and Tumbleoff on their sturdy machine, she fought tooth and nail to keep within striking distance of the Italian bike. She drifted her bike through bends with screeching tyres; she roared down the longer straights till the wind in her face drew back her cheeks in an alarming grimace. She had never experienced such exhilaration in her life.

Mr Edwards was experiencing exhilaration too, but for him it was mixed with blind terror. If you are a Headteacher probably the most frightening thing that ever happens to you is meeting parents on parents' evenings. But motorbike and sidecar racing was even more frightening than that.

'Come on, Baldilocks! Don't just sit there like a bank manager at a funeral. Lean out or you'll have us in the ditch!' yelled Vera to him above the crackle of the twin exhausts. 'The further the better!'

As they swept into a long right-hander he sat up a bit and leaned gingerly out over the sidecar's wheel. It made him feel rather sick, and the wind was chill where it channelled between the lapels of his best grey suit.

'THAT'S IT,' shouted Vera encouragingly. *'Think of the credit you can bring to your school!'*

This seemed to do the trick. It touched a spark deep within the Headteacher's bald head, and a determined smile lit his face. He decided to throw caution to the winds. 'What the heck,' he thought to himself. 'I'm only ever going to be in one Grand Prix in my life so I might as well make the most of it – so what if I do something wrong and we fly off the track – at least we'll go out in a blaze of glory. If you're going to do something you might as well do it to the best of your ability. At least I will know that I tried!'

'That's more like it!' yelled Vera with approval in her voice, as Mr Edwards threw himself from side to side, the afternoon sun glinting occasionally on the top of his glossy red head.

'THIS IS SLURY TALKER and we have a

*sensation here on lap five. The Russians have over-
taken the Italians and are in the lead! So it's Russia first
followed by Italy then Mrs Pratt closely followed by Aryton
Sennapod from Brazil!'*

Slury Talker was right. The Captain had left his
braking a little late as he approached a tight left-
hand bend, and Igor Blimey had nipped into the
space left on the inside of the track.

'NOW LOOK WHAT YOU'VE GONE
AND DONE, CHEQUE!' roared the Captain
to the cowering Dud Cheque. 'Pesky Ruskies!
Come on, Cheque, there's five thousand quid at
stake!'

Although it had not been Dud's fault that they
had lost the lead, it was true that he wasn't performing as well as he might have. The Italian racing suit
was getting in the way. The body was so big that the
collar came up from time to time and threatened to
cover his face, and the sleeves were so long that they
came over his gloves and he couldn't be sure what
he was holding on to.

The Captain threw him a sidewards glance on the
next long straight: 'Pull yourself together, man!
Sort your suit out and get rid of all those wrinkles –
you don't look like an Italian racing driver, you look
more like an elephant's bum. If we're rumbled we'll
end up in gaol!'

'OK, Guv,' shouted Dud. He'd already ended up

in gaol on several occasions in his life, and he didn't want to do it again.

'And we're going to have to do something about those Ruskies!' snarled the Captain, bending low over the petrol tank. Actually the Captain did not relish the idea of doing something about the Russians.

'*It's still the Russians in the lead!*' squawked Slurry Talker. 'But it's anyone's race. There's a long way to go! It's *so exciting*!!'

One person who wasn't finding it at all exciting

was Wally Pratt. He was sitting in the store-room of the ABC Garage team's pit with his hands and ankles tied together and a gag in his mouth.

16

Wally Pratt

Above the sound of the motorbike engines roaring round the track outside, Wally suddenly thought he heard a scratching sound. He strained his ears in the semi-darkness of the tiny store-room.

Yes, sure enough, there it was again.

He was sitting on the floor and had managed to get moderately comfortable with his back against the wall of the pit garage, and his feet straight out in front of him.

The scratching turned to a tapping noise; it was coming from the tiny window above his head. Though the ropes round his legs and arms restricted his movement, Wally turned his head and could tell that there was someone at the window. He could see the shape of a head outside and the shadow it cast cut out some of the light.

There was another tap on the glass. Wally could plainly see the shape of a hand.

'UG!' he called, as loudly as the gag would permit. 'YUG! HULPP!'

Then Wally heard a voice: 'Wally, are you there?'
It was Ginger Tom's voice, Wally was sure of it –
but the window was at least six feet off the ground,
and Ginger was only knee high to a grasshopper.
What was going on?

If Wally had been in the paddock outside the back of the pits, and not locked up in a store-room, he would have seen the simple solution to this puzzle. Ginger was kneeling on Bean Pole's shoulders.

The three boys had done as Vera Pratt had directed. The moment the race had begun they had gone to the back of the ABC Garage pit.

Checking first that the coast was clear they had tried to open the back door, but it was obviously bolted on the inside. Then they had decided to try to look through the small window that was set high in the back wall.

'Come on, Ginger. Get on my shoulders,' said Bean Pole. In the absence of Wally Pratt, Bean Pole was the small group's natural leader.

After a lot of struggling and wobbling, Ginger Tom managed to reach the window and peer in. He covered the side of his face with his hand to cut out reflections: 'I can't see much,' he reported to Bean Pole and Bill Stickers. 'It's pretty dark in there – I think it must be the store-room at the back, like in Mrs Pratt's.'

Then he tapped on the window, and shouted for Wally. Ginger Tom thought he heard a faint reply. 'Hey, I think he's in here!' he said. 'But we'll never get the window open – it's definitely locked.'

'I think we'd better break the glass,' said Bean

Pole, and Bill Stickers passed a handy piece of brick up to Ginger Tom.

'Watch out, Wally,' shouted Ginger through the glass. 'I'm going to bust the window!'

Luckily, the sound of the motorbikes as they roared round the track meant that no one heard the crash and tinkle of breaking glass.

Wally heard it all right and his legs were instantly covered in a shower of broken glass.

'Wally! Are you in there?!' asked Ginger Tom eagerly through the hole where the pane of glass had been.

'UG!' said Wally. 'I UM!'

'I can't see him, but he's in here OK,' said Tom to the two boys outside. 'I think he's been drugged or something: are you OK, Wally?'

'UG,' said Wally again.

Ginger carefully removed the remaining sharp slivers of glass from the window frame. 'Bean Pole,' he said. 'Hold me very still, I'm going to try to get my head through this hole and see if I can see him.'

Bill Stickers helped to steady Bean Pole, and Ginger put his head on one side and carefully eased it through the small gaping hole.

Looking down the wall below the window Ginger Tom could just make Wally out in the gloom. 'Hang on, Wally,' he said, and he withdrew his head slowly and slithered off Bean Pole's shoulders to the ground.

'He's in there all right, on the floor; and he's gagged and tied up,' said Ginger to his two friends. 'It's too small for me to get in, let alone get Wally out! What can we do?'

'He won't have a hope of getting out of there while he's tied up,' observed Bean Pole with a frown on his face. 'Couldn't he use a sharp piece of the broken glass to cut the rope round his wrists – then he might be able to untie himself and get the door open somehow.'

'Brilliant!' said Bill Stickers. 'Go on, Ginger, back you go and tell him.'

So Ginger Tom climbed back on to Bean Pole's aching shoulders and spoke again to Wally.

'Hey, Wally, we think you should try to get a piece of sharp glass and cut the rope off your wrists. Look – there's a large bit just in front of you.' Ginger could see it lying on the floor just by Wally's knee. 'The guys in this pit are certainly up to something. Your mum thinks they pinched her petrol, and you'll never guess what has happened to old Edwards! His hair has fallen off. It's a wig – and the men in this pit have nicked it! He looks really odd – but your mum sprayed his head with red gloss paint and he's in her sidecar in the race!'

Wally hardly had time to think about such extraordinary things. He shuffled on his bottom until he reached the large triangular piece of glass that Ginger Tom had referred to. He managed to pick it up with his fingertips, and with much care, and not a little anxiety, he lined it up with the stout rope that Dud Cheque had tied round his wrists.

Wally began to move the glass to and fro. He could feel it beginning to sever the strands of the rope.

After much effort and a little time the ropes that held his wrists so tightly suddenly parted. In a moment Wally tore the gag from his mouth: 'I've done it!' he exclaimed to Ginger Tom who was watching the proceedings from above. 'Hang on while I get these ropes off my legs too!'

It didn't take Wally Pratt very long to free his legs.

'Well done, Wally – can you get through the door?' asked Ginger.

'I doubt it – I heard the key turn in the lock the moment they shut me in here. I'll try though,' said Wally bravely.

'You're killing my shoulders!' said Bean Pole to Ginger Tom.

'Wally – Bean Pole needs a rest,' said Ginger and he slid once more to the ground.

With no one at the window the store-room had more light in it. Wally rubbed his sore ankles and wrists, and went over to the door. He turned the handle and pushed, but it was obviously locked.

For some strange reason Wally suddenly remembered the words of his Headteacher Mr Edwards: he remembered the warnings about doing something intelligent, and showing initiative, and improving his performance in general.

'OK, Mr Edwards,' he said to himself. 'I'll show you!'

17

Something Fishy

He put his eye to the keyhole. It was obviously blocked with something – Wally hoped it was the key. He looked round to see what implements and escape aids the store-room held.

It was almost empty: unlike his mother's pit store there were no tools. There were a few old tyres in the far corner, a lot of litter on the floor, and not much else.

Among the litter was a paper bag. Wally flattened it out and slid it carefully under the door beneath the keyhole, leaving just a corner of it on his side of the door. He prayed silently that there was no one outside in the garage who would see what he was up to. Then he searched the grimy floor of the store: he knew exactly what he was looking for – a piece of wire, or stick, or anything that would fit into the keyhole.

Beneath some shelving he found something that would do: a pencil with a broken point. He picked up a piece of glass and used it to shave the pencil to a thin stick.

Then he stuck it into the keyhole and wiggled and pushed it. With a clang he heard the key fall to the ground outside the door. It was music to his ears!

He knelt on the floor behind the door, and the moment he moved the paper bag he sensed that his plan was working. The key was lying on the paper outside the door.

He inched the bag slowly towards him and fortunately there was quite a large gap beneath the door. Bending low Wally could actually see the key. Pulling carefully he eased it towards him, and using the sharpened pencil he finally managed to prise the key beneath the door and into his hands.

It only took him a second to get the key into the store-room lock, turn it, and release himself from his temporary dungeon.

Wally checked to see that the O'Reilly brothers were not around, and then he gently slid back the two bolts on the garage back door. He carefully turned the handle and opened it.

As the afternoon sunlight flooded into the dingy garage, its beam fell on a brown wig lying at Wally's feet. It was Mr Edwards' wig – lying where Dud Cheque had kicked it. Wally did an intelligent and enterprising thing: he picked it up and stuffed it into his trouser pocket, then he nipped outside into the sunlight and freedom.

Bean Pole and Ginger and Bill Stickers greeted him like a long lost comrade in arms: they slapped him on the back and shook him by the hand.

'Come on, Wally, let's get back to your mum's pit,' said Bean Pole enthusiastically. 'You'll be safer there.' They started walking at a brisk pace.

'I don't get it,' said Wally as they went. 'If Mum says the crew from the garage pinched her petrol, and they kidnapped me – where are they now? Their bike conked out yesterday and they withdrew from the race. Why would they be so keen to stop us winning?'

'Search me,' said Bill Stickers, and Bean Pole

added: 'Anyway, your mum can still win – she and old Edwards were about third just now.'

What Bean Pole said was true. Out on the track a small bunch of leading bikes had broken clear of the rest. The Russians were in the lead closely followed by the Captain and Dud Cheque on the Italian machine, with Vera Pratt never far behind them.

When it was safe to do so, the boys crossed the pit lane and mingled with a small group of race fans on the edge of the track. Bean Pole, being the tallest, looked round from time to time to check that no O'Reillys were in sight.

'GO ON, MUM!' yelled Wally as the leaders swept past them at breakneck speed. The other boys cheered too.

'Do you know something?' said Wally in a hoarse whisper to the others as the leading bikes disappeared into the distance. 'There's something fishy about those Italians in second place . . . I spent most of yesterday evening following them round the track and I got a good look at them. Somehow today they don't look right . . .'

18

Heading for Victory

'This is Slury Talker at the Motorbike and Sidecar Grand Prix, and with the race reaching its half-way stage we still have the Russians leading. But it's anybody's race! It's still *terribly exciting*!'

This was true. You could have thrown a blanket over the leading bunch of bikes, they were so close to each other. This was particularly so in the bends, corners and chicanes; on longer straights Igor Blimey and Captain Smoothy-Smythe had a small power advantage over Vera Pratt and both of them managed to pull away from her. It was Vera's skill and bravery in leaving her braking to the last split second that made the difference, and when she did brake she pulled the lever at her right hand so hard that beads of blood formed beneath the nicely mani-cured fingernails deep within her red leather racing gauntlet.

'I say, Mrs Pratt . . .' said Mr Edwards as they swung into a small chicane. 'We seem to be doing OK!'

'Yes!' yelled back Vera through gritted teeth. 'If only I can get between these two in front. It's difficult to pick them off when they're so close together!' She opened the throttle wide and sunk down low behind the tiny windshield. 'Lean out as much as you possibly can – it's cornering that's the secret in this game!'

On the bike ahead of them another shouted conversation was going on:

'Cheque, you half-wit! Lean out more!'

'I'm doing me best, Guv!'

'Well, it's not good enough! How the blinking blazes can we catch these Russians if you sit there like a sheep on the lavatory. You're not here to enjoy the view, buddy boy! You're here to help me win five thousand quid!'

Secretly Captain Smoothy-Smythe was quite pleased with the way things were going. The Italian bike was a masterpiece of engineering – far superior to the O'Reilly Special that lay rusting in a nearby ditch. He sensed its immense power beneath him. 'If I can just get level with those Russians,' thought the Captain to himself, 'I think I could get ahead – especially if no one's looking!'

A wicked sneer lit his lips and moustache.

The Russians were also shouting remarks to each other, but in Russian, so I won't bother to write them down.

Five laps later the Captain saw his chance. Vera Pratt had missed a gear coming out of a sharp left-hander, and was a good ten lengths behind him. As he slipped the bike into top he turned and spoke to Dud Cheque: 'Hold very tight on this long straight, Cheque, and keep down – I'm going into business with these Ruskies!'

They were right out in the country now, where the track cut straight through a small pinewood. The Captain tucked his bike in behind the Russians' back wheel and then, picking his moment with care, he opened the throttle as far as it would go and slowly drew alongside their sidecar.

Tumbleoff turned his head towards the Captain in surprise, but in that split second Captain Smoothy-Smythe, villain and cheat, put his hand inside his tight Italian racing suit and extracted from its depths a striped football sock. It was filled to the top with heavy wet sand.

The two machines were now side by side and practically touching. The Captain swung the sock round his head a couple of times like a medieval knight on horseback with a spiked ball and chain, and then he sloshed it with all his might round the head of Mr Tumbleoff. It wrapped itself round like a striped boa constrictor, and Tumbleoff lived up to his name. Shouting a Russian swear-word that we couldn't print here even if we knew what it was, he

fell from the sidecar in a bewildered tangle of arms and legs. He bounced twice before going out of sight into the small pinewood. He was soon followed by Igor Blimey and the magnificent Soviet motorbike.

The Captain threw back his head in a demonic laugh. He was in the lead once more, and heading for victory!

19

Vera Pratt Pulls Out the Stops

'Look at that!' exclaimed Bean Pole as the leaders swept past them on the next lap. 'The Italians are in the lead again!'

'The Russians must have conked out or something,' said Bill.

'Your mum is second!' added Ginger Tom excitedly.

'HANG ON!' said Wally, his mouth and eyes widening in amazement. 'I've got it. Those aren't the Italians who were riding yesterday, I'm certain of it!'

'What do you mean?' asked Bill Stickers.

'Well, I spent most of yesterday evening in Mum's sidecar following the Italian team round the track. I got plenty of time to look at them – their sidecar man was much bigger than that bloke: he had a much better style too. *I reckon that bike is being ridden by those two creeps from the ABC Garage!*'

'You're joking!' said Bean Pole in disbelief.

'I'm not! And they need stopping.' Wally looked

thoughtful for a moment or two. 'Wait here,' he said quietly. 'I'll be back in a minute.'

He nipped back across the pit lane and went into his mother's pit garage. A second or two later he emerged stuffing something into his trouser pocket. He ran up to the boys. 'Right,' he said. 'Follow me, and be quick!'

As you know, Wally Pratt is normally a slow mover. However, I did point out earlier that in an emergency he could produce an impressive burst of speed. This was an emergency.

He set off through the crowded pit area and ran across the paddock that backed on to it. Then he and his breathless companions climbed over a fence, crossed a small car park and soon arrived at the quiet part of the track, out in the country in the pinewood where Igor Blimey and Tumbleoff had so recently come to grief. No spectators gathered there because the long straight was the least spectacular point on the track.

When they got there the boys were all out of breath; they were just getting it back again when they heard an announcement over the track loud-speakers:

'Only three more laps to go, and it's the Italians leading the field, with Mrs Pratt the local entrant in second place.'

'What are we going to do?' Ginger Tom panted to Wally.

'I've thought of something – just wait and see,' said Wally Pratt. And the four looked anxiously down the track for the leading bikes.

At that moment Vera and Mr Edwards were rocketing along in front of the grandstand. She was pleased to have got the Italian bike in view again but was surprised to see that the Russian one seemed to have disappeared.

'Where are those Russians?' yelled Mr Edwards who'd noticed it too.

'They must have gone off the track somewhere,' replied Vera Pratt.

Being a capable and determined sort of lady, Vera knew that the messed-up gear change a couple of laps ago had been her own fault and that the only thing she could do to put matters right would be to go all out for victory. She knew that it was worth taking every risk, to drive to the very limit of her skill, determination and courage: 'Hold tight, Baldilocks! We've only three laps left and I'm going to pull out all the stops!'

As she said it they entered a tight right-hand bend, and she and Mr Edwards leaned in unison over the sidecar. A new spirit of teamwork suffused their performance, and for the next two laps they broke every record in the book. Slury Talker could hardly believe his stop-watch: 'This is *amazing*! *Incredible*! The greatest riding *I've ever seen*!' he squealed.

They powered through back markers like a pike through a shoal of minnows, and drifted through bends till their tyres smoked. Mr Edwards' eyes watered, and if he'd had time to stop and think about it he'd have realized that if he had been wearing his wig it would have blown off long ago.

But all thoughts and doubts and fears were lost in the common purpose to catch and beat the Italians.

So, two laps later, when Captain Smoothy-Smythe whizzed past the boys in the pinewood Wally's mum was only a metre behind him.

'She's going like the wind, your mum,' remarked Bill Stickers in amazement. Wally nodded, and secretly longed to be there in the sidecar, beside his remarkable ton-up mother.

'Watch out, Guv, she's gaining on us!' shouted Dud Cheque in the Italian sidecar.

'Don't worry about her,' snarled the Captain. 'There's only one lap to go, and if she's got any nearer when we come through this wood on the next lap she'll get the jolly old Russian treatment!'

20

The Last Lap

'HERE IT IS – the last lap!' squeaked Slury Talker into his microphone. *'And the Italians still lead but with Mrs Pratt the local hero right on their tail! This is so exciting! The crowd are willing her on. Just listen to them! Amazing!'*

Out in the pinewood there was a strange hush. The number of bikes still in the race had gradually dwindled during the afternoon as engines blew up, tyres punctured, and riders made small mistakes that sent them careering into the straw bales and piles of tyres around the track. For what seemed like several minutes the long straight through the wood was empty. The track lay there like a broad black ribbon, waiting for the leading bikes to roar over it for the last time that day.

Wally Pratt, Bean Pole, Ginger Tom and Bill Stickers focused their eyes on the distant left-hand bend, and waited.

Would Vera Pratt and the brave Mr Edwards be

in the lead this time? Or would the Italian bike have pulled away from her?

The air was still, the birds fell silent: the world held its breath.

Then they saw them. The two bikes were coming through the bend almost side by side. It was impossible to be certain which one was actually in front.

They began the straight together, the two riders matching each other gear change for gear change. Wally's mum was on the far side of the track. The bikes were separated by centimetres.

'She's gaining on us, Guv!' shouted Dud with panic in his voice. 'She's going to overtake!'

'Damn!' snarled the Captain. 'And she's going on the outside!'

This meant that Vera was trying to overtake on the sidecar side of the Captain's outfit, and this in turn meant that instead of him being able to slosh the rival *passenger* with a sock full of sand, as had happened to the Russians, the Captain would have to adjust his tactics and get Dud Cheque to slug Vera Pratt herself.

'Here, Cheque!' shouted the Captain as he opened the throttle to its fullest extent. '*TAKE THIS!*'

The Captain pulled the football sock from the front of his suit and handed it to Cheque. 'Wait till you can see the whites of her eyes, then slosh her round the jolly old gob with it!'

Dud Cheque took the sock – no easy task at the speed they were travelling. 'And, Cheque . . .' snarled the Captain, his eyes wide with fury and desperation. 'If you mess this up I shall personally dismantle you and feed you to my dog . . .'

The two leading bikes were not very far from the boys when they saw, to their horror, that the Italian passenger was sitting up and was swirling a football sock full of sand round his head.

Vera Pratt's bike was exactly alongside the other. There was no doubting the leading passenger's intentions. 'LOOK, WALLY!' shouted Bean Pole – 'That guy is trying to cosh your mum!'

'Right!' said Wally, and he went into action. He put his hand in his pocket and brought out something brown and hairy.

'What on earth is that?' said Bill Stickers.

'It's old Edwards' wig. I found it in the ABC pit garage. But I've done something to it.'

Wally pulled his arm back and lobbed the wig directly into the path of the Italian motorbike and sidecar. It landed on the tarmac with a splat.

'What do you mean?' asked Ginger Tom, incredulously.

'I found his wig on the floor, and I took it into Mum's pit just now and soaked it in engine oil. I thought it might come in handy as a skid pad, now GET DOWN!'

The four boys lay in the grass, their hands over

their ears and their eyes fixed on the wig which lay like a large squashed hedgehog on the track in front of them.

Captain Smoothy-Smythe was so busy shouting at Dud Cheque, and trying to manoeuvre his bike and sidecar so that Vera Pratt was in range of the swinging sock full of sand, that he didn't even notice the dark shape on the road ahead.

The moment the bike's front wheel hit it he wished that he had.

The oily wig was as slippery as an eel in washing-up liquid. The front wheel slid to the left, Dud Cheque lost his balance, and the football sock cosh went spinning harmlessly into the air.

The sleek machine hit the kerb at full speed: it shot across a grass verge, went through a small fence, and entered the depths of the pinewood several feet in the air.

It came down in a small boggy clearing with a resounding *SPLASH!*

As it happened, it landed very close to where the two Russians had so recently ended their after-noon's racing.

Igor Blimey and Tumbleoff had only just re-covered their senses. They had helped each other to their feet, inspected each other for cuts and bruises, and had discovered that, surprisingly, they were both alive and well.

The same could not have been said of their

motorbike and sidecar which lay in a tangled heap against a tree, so they had decided to leave it where it was and start the long walk back to the pits.

They were surprised and rather delighted when they were joined by the sleek Italian machine, and the two individuals in ill-fitting racing suits who had been so obviously responsible for Russia's undeserved defeat.

As Captain Smoothy-Smythe and Dud Cheque sat in the cold, wet, marshy water, gathering their thoughts and muttering very rude words, the two Russians emerged into the clearing through the trees with a mixture of anger and glee on their faces, their sleeves rolled up, and their fists tightly clenched.

I'll leave it to you to imagine what happened next.

21

The Chequered Flag

With the track suddenly clear ahead of them, Vera Pratt and Mr Edwards had a simple task.

Like the motorcycling genius she is, Vera steered her splendid machine to certain victory. She sailed through the last remaining corners like a dream – Mr Edwards matching her move for move. They acted in unison, like something on *Come Dancing*.

They took the chequered flag to the roar of the mighty crowd; as they crossed the line they both raised their arms in acknowledgement of their own achievement. The grandstand rose in joyous salute, and Slury Talker got so excited he nearly wet himself.

De-accelerating, and with a kindly smile on her face, Vera leaned across to her team-mate: 'You were very good, Baldy. You don't really have my Wally's weight or experience, but you picked it up very quickly, especially for a forty-two-year-old.'

'Thank you, Mrs Pratt. I must say you're a wizard on this bike: it really was quite an

experience. I haven't had so much fun since last year's nativity play.'

The crowd were still waving and shouting and cheering.

'Come on – we'll have to do a lap of honour now,' said Vera and, settling back with the engine merely ticking over, they began to cruise round the course for one last extra lap.

Every group of fans they passed gave them an extra loud cheer. They went gently through all the early bends, and the chicane, and headed out into the country. As they entered the long straight through the woods they noticed a small group of fans standing on the edge of the wood.

'Good heavens!' said Mr Edwards. 'I think that's young Wallace and his friends.'

Sure enough, as Vera brought the bike to a halt beside the group it turned out to be the four boys.

'WALLY!' said Vera. 'Are you all right? What happened?'

'Oh, I got captured by the mob from the ABC Garage, Mum, but the lads here helped me to escape.'

'Well done, boys – a credit to the school!' chipped in Mr Edwards with a smile.

'What are you doing out here then?' asked Vera, amazed.

'Well, we had to fix the so-called Italians: you see, they weren't the Carburetti brothers at all – they were those crooks from the garage,' explained Wally Pratt.

'So Wally fixed them,' added Bean Pole.

'Fixed them?' Mr Edwards didn't understand.

'Yeah. We could see that they were going to try to knock you off the track so I lobbed Mr Edwards' wig, soaked in oil, under their front tyre.'

'It worked a treat,' added Bean Pole again. He was very proud of his friend Wally.

'MY LOOK-TEN-YEARS-YOUNGER HAIR-PIECE!' Mr Edwards put his hand to his glossy red head in despair. 'I'd quite forgotten about it in the excitement! You wouldn't have any idea where it is now, would you?' He looked worried.

'It's here, where I chucked it,' said Wally, and he bent down and peeled the oily wig from the surface of the road. It looked more like a squished hedgehog than ever.

'Thank heavens!' said Mr Edwards with a relieved smile. He put the tacky remains of the wig on his head, and smoothed it down to cover the gloss red paint. Spikes of greasy hair stood up in all directions.

'I don't know how I could have gone through the prize ceremony without it!' said the happy Mr Edwards, though he looked more like a punk rocker than a schoolteacher.

Then Vera beckoned the boys to get on the bike and sidecar, and with a gentle burst on the throttle they all continued on their lap of honour together.

22

Rewards!

The sun was already well below the topmost branches of the oak and beech trees that surrounded the paddock behind the pits, when Colonel Thundering-Blunderer walked forward to present a magnificent silver cup and an envelope containing a cheque for five thousand pounds to Mrs Vera Pratt.

Then she and Mr Edwards stood on a podium, alongside Aryton Sennapod from Brazil, and a team from the Isle of Man who had come third. They all had their photographs taken and were interviewed by the breathless Slury Talker.

Slowly the huge crowd dispersed. They all agreed that it had been a great day's racing, and that in the end the best outfit, led by one of the world's most extraordinary mothers, had won.

As evening fell, and sunset's rosy light threw long shadows over the pit area, Vera Pratt tidied away her tools and bits and pieces, helped by her dear son Wally, and his friends Bean Pole, Bill Stickers and Ginger Tom.

When the pit was clear of all her things, the boys

got on the bike and sidecar, and with a single kick
Vera fired the engine into life.

'Time for home,' she said.

At the entrance to the race track she was spotted
by Mr Edwards who had gone to check that the
children responsible for clearing litter from the car
parks had done a good job.

He walked over to the bike and sidecar. 'I must
say,' he said. 'You boys put in a good day's work
today, you can be proud of yourselves.'

'Oh, come on, Mr Edwards!' exclaimed Mrs Pratt
turning off the engine. 'What about you?! You were
magnificent in the sidecar. In fact I've been thinking
it over. I feel that half the prize money is really
yours.' She took the envelope from her red racing
suit pocket.

'Mrs Pratt . . .' said the Headteacher firmly, 'I
won't hear of it. All the money is yours – if half *was*
due to me I would give it to you anyway – as a small
payment for my thanks that you and the boys here
can keep a secret!'

The evening sunlight danced amongst the oily
spikes of his wig as he said it.

'Thank you,' said Vera with a smile. 'We understand.' And kicking the engine into life once more,
she eased the throttle open and headed for home.

The next day was the last day of term, and at the end
of it Wally Pratt proudly presented his mother with

his school report. On the page that the Headteacher
fills in it simply said:

*Wallace is a star pupil at St Bernard's. When threatened
he shows outstanding energy, initiative and intelligence.
He is* A CREDIT TO THE SCHOOL.

AUTHOR'S NOTE: *Three weeks after the end of this story Captain Smoothy-Smythe and Mr Dudley Cheque came out of hospital.*